White Fox Blues

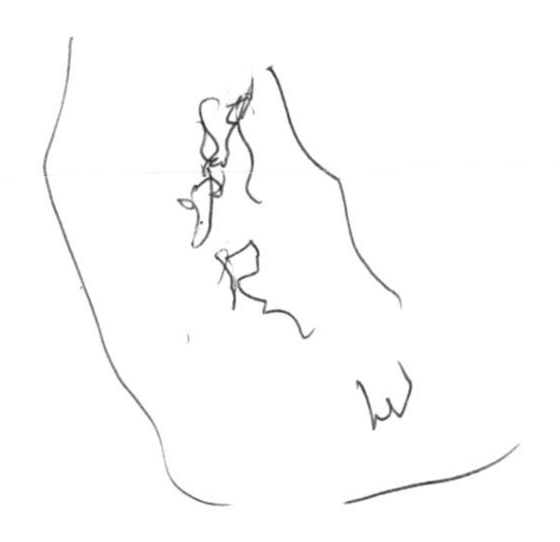

Nathaniel Robert Winters

•

BUFFALO PRINTINGCOMPANY

Napa Valley California

For information please address rwinters2350@yahoo.com

Authors note:

The time line and facts introduced in each chapter are factual as are the major characters in the War with one exception. I changed the timing of the movie *Casablanca.* It came out three months after Operation Torch but I couldn't resist including the dialog of one of my favorite movies. I claim poetic license after all this book is a work of fiction.

Chapter 1

2018

The whole endeavor started when Sara was given one of those heredity background tests as a gift for her twenty-first birthday. Her DNA took her on a trip back thousands of years to Eastern European Ashkenazi Jewish roots, most of which she already knew about. It also led her to many relatives whose stories ended in Concentration Camps during World War II.

Almost buried in the mountain of paperwork was the name Rose Cohen, of Switzerland, the sister of Sara's great-grandmother. None of the family had heard of this mystery women. Sara's great-grandmother died just two years earlier at the age of ninety-two.

This apparent gap in their family history sent Sara's parents on a frantic internet search. Sure enough, after days of hunting, the once unknown Swiss Miss, Rose Cohen, was found still living in Zurich. She admitted she lost contact with her sister after WWII and knew nothing about her American relatives.

My name is Roger Raintree and Sara has been my best friend since...well...since forever. Our parents were friends before we were born. Because it was Sara's birthday present that discovered Rose, she was picked to go to Europe and make personal contact with her great-aunt. Sara asked me to go with her. Lucky me.

Sara just finished her junior year at Berkeley. I was a year younger, a year behind her at Cal and we shared an apartment together. We never dated each other, ever. We were really good friends almost like sister and brother.

Neither of us had been to Europe before. Our parents thought we should use our summer vacation, go to Switzerland and learn about Rose.

I googled Rose Cohen but found next to nothing about the woman. I had a feeling she was hiding something, maybe something important.

Chapter 2

June – July, 2018

The whole tribe of our two houses saw Sara and me off at the airport in St. Louis. With all the hugs and kisses behind us, we proceeded through security, found our gate and boarded the over-sized jet aircraft.

As we fell into our coach seats, Sara grabbed my hand holding on hard. She said, "I get really nervous during take-off."

"I have kind of a mantra I use that works for me to calm down. Want to try it?"

"Sure," she said, her voice sounding an octave higher than normal.

"When the plane starts speeding down the runway, I yell "thrust" to myself over and over and on take-off, I silently sing the Air Force song."

The big jet moved into position, the engines started to roar. The brakes came off and we rolled forward picking up speed.

Sara and I shouted "thrust, thrust, thrust, thrust" and as we became airborne, we sang out-loud. "Off we go into the wide blue yonder…"

Of course, few could hear us over the screaming of four jet engines. We almost swallowed our chewing gum laughing so hard. Sara let go of my hand and patted me on the leg, "That totally worked."

I had no mantra for the eight-hour cramped plane ride to London in coach.

We scheduled only one day in London and rode one of those double-decker tour buses to see Big Ben and Parliament where Winston Churchill saved western democracy. We got off the bus at the Tower Bridge and the infamous Tower of London, known as a place where heads were lost, including Anne Boleyn's.

The next day we crossed the channel and went on a pilgrimage to Normandy. My great-grandfather took part in the D-day invasion and lucky for me, he survived, so the battle-ground memorial felt very real as though my history book had come alive.

Looking down from the German seawall on top of the cliffs to the beach below, it's amazing any Americans survived and yet somehow, they were able to win the battle. At the graveyard, looking at the lines of crosses and stars, the price those soldiers paid for freedom left a powerful impression on me.

We went on to Paris for Bastille Day. That night, we got an amazing eyeful of fireworks over the Eiffel Tower. Music played from gigantic speakers matching notes to the explosions as thousands in the streets danced along. A *wow* moment I'll never forget.

The following day we toured the Louvre and the Napoleonic Museum. Sara fell in love with the Louvre and I did too but I have to say, I was disappointed with the Mona Lisa; somehow I was expecting more.

Being a history major, I felt at home at Napoleon's Museum, Sara not so much.

Our last day in Paris we took a tour of Versailles with castle grounds that went on forever and a ballroom painted in real gold. No wonder Louis lost his head over the place.

It would appear both England and France had a history of people getting their heads chopped off, and the French even invented a machine to do it better and quicker. I would like to think humanity has evolved from the horrors of earlier centuries but the Nazis proved we may be devolving.

Early morning on July 18th we caught the train to Zurich. All along the tracks, mountain scenery proved to be breathtaking. About noon when we arrived, Rose greeted us, Sara's picture in hand. Mrs. Cohen wore an immaculate long brown skirt and vest, with a matching scarf sweeping back her silver hair.

"Don't worry about your luggage. My driver, Phil, will take care of it," Rose said as Phil ushered us into the back seat of a large Mercedes Benz.

I said, "Nice car."

Rose said, "This thing? Every taxi cab driver has one of these."

"What car would you say is nice?" I asked her.

"In the 1950's I had a pink Cadillac convertible with those long fins; wasn't very useful in winter but in summer, that car was the cat's meow. Are you kids hungry?"

"I'm famished," I said

Sara said, "I could eat."

"Good, the cook is making schnitzel. We will be home in five minutes."

Sara asked, "Aunt Rose what happened between you and Iris, that we didn't even know about you?"

"That my dear child, is a long story."

Chapter 3

Rose's Story as told to Roger and Sara.

(All foreign conversations were translated by Rose Cohen.)

March 1938

Marc Cohen trusted only his daughter Rose, no one else, with good reason. His fortune spread throughout many countries and much of it came from ill-gotten methods.

Marc Cohen appeared unimpressive in every way. Standing five feet two inches and weighing in at 145 pounds, you might miss him in a crowd. He wore an inexpensive suit off the rack, and smelled like garlic, tobacco and Old Spice.

He liked blending in, not to be noticed, having people believe he was just another one of the guys. No one would know that he was worth billions. He owned large tracts of land in many countries. Amassing tons of gold bullion and cash, lots of cash, stored in Swiss banks, the banks of his homeland.

He was a bootlegger during America's not so noble experiment with prohibition. Working out of the port of Naples, Italy, his shipping line smuggled Italian and French wines and Cuban rum to gang contacts in the United States. His clients included Italian mobsters; also a Jewish importer by the name of Meyer Lansky.

Since the end of Prohibition, Cohen continued to legally export wine, rum and other liquor using the same contacts.

With Mussolini controlling Italy, making it more difficult for Mafia bosses in Naples, a Swiss business man like Cohen became even more valuable to his associates.

It had become very dangerous to be a Jew in Hitler's Germany. Unemployment, arrests, assault and even murder lurked, as Jews faced a new reality in their Nazi nightmare. That evil was about to spread to Austria as Germany annexed its neighbor without even a taste of resistance.

Meyer Lansky and Marc Cohen came up with the idea to smuggle Jews out of the expanding German empire with their booze shipments, using Cuba as a temporary drop zone, until the right palms in Washington could be greased.

George, Lansky's representative, was going over details of the plan. "So, basically you will finance your end and my boss will take care of the American costs. But we split the Cuban expenses, right?"

"That works for us, won't it Rose?"

"Yes Dad, we can handle that."

At fifteen years-old, Rose Cohen already started to show the curves that would make her an alluring woman. Despite her youth she kept the books and ran her father's business.

Rose was only one quarter Jewish but she knew if she were German and not Swiss that any percentage of Jewish blood would be enough for the Nazi's.

"Okay, no written contracts. From our mouths to God's ears. Deal?" Mr. Cohen said.

"Deal," said George.

The two men shook hands.

Chapter 4

April 1938

Innsbruck sat tucked in a lovely river valley below the grandeur of the snow-capped Alps Mountains. Spring flowers bloomed setting the small city ablaze in color. The fairy tale backdrop was disillusioned by the marching of German soldiers through the city center. Austrians welcomed them with cheers and the waving of Nazi flags.

Just blocks away, Rose pulled the chimes at the front gate of the Cohen walled family estate. The large stone house had a castle-like turret rising from the second floor. Her sister Iris darted out to greet her. They had been apart for a year, the longest separation of their lives. After hugs they took inventory of each other.

Iris said, "Let me see, long blond hair, baby blue eyes, breasts getting bigger, well you're even more beautiful than the last time I saw you."

Rose laughed, looking at her mirror image. They were twins. "Well thanks, you don't look so bad yourself."

"Hello Rose," her mother said as she strolled out to greet her long absent daughter. Katherine was dressed impeccably, with a long brown skirt and vest matching her hair, but Rose noticed a touch of gray she had not seen before.

The two kissed cheeks with an absence of warmth, not actually touching. Rose said, "Mother, it's good to see you. You look well."

"Thank you, how is your rotten father?"

"He is worried about you."

"Well, that's a first," Katherine said. "Come in, are you hungry?"

"I could eat," Rose acknowledged. It was a long train ride."

"Good, the cook is making some schnitzel, come, you are too skinny."

"Stop it, I look exactly like Iris," Rose countered.

"She is too skinny as well."

The girls exchanged a look.

They walked through an immense hallway past the dining room and into the kitchen where Rose ran into the arms of the family cook.

"Oh, Hilde it's so good to see you. How have you been?"

"Hi Rosy, I've been good. How are you?"

"I'm doing very well, but I sure do miss your cooking. The schnitzel smells so good. My mouth is watering."

"Eat darling,'' Hilde said, and she served the three women each a big plate of food.

They retreated to the dining room and Rose said, "It will get too dangerous for you to stay, with Hitler's henchman taking over the government. You two must leave while you still can."

"What about our home?" Her Mom asked. "We can't leave our home."

Rose shrugged her shoulders. We will sell it."

"This estate has been in our family for generations. My older brother Joseph died defending Austria in the Great War," Katherine reminded her daughter.

"And the Baron would be disgusted by the capitulation of the Austrian Government now," Rose said. "The Germans took over the country without a shot fired to defend it."

Iris said, “Mom things have changed. I will be forced to wear the Jewish star on my clothing and some kids at school are calling me ‘rich bitch Jew.’”

Rose said, “You are risking your lives if you stay.”

“Where would we go?” Katherine asked.

“Father has family in America, St. Louis, Missouri. They will sponsor getting you a visa,” Rose said.

“Stay with your father’s family? No way,” Katherine said.

“Mother, that is the only way to get you two a visa,” Rose said.

Iris asked, “Did you see the storm troopers goose-stepping into town today? It’s a nightmare.”

Katherine looked defeated. “All right, we will go on vacation and see this St. Louis. If things change here, we can come home.”

Chapter 5

1918 -1938

Katherine Wineheim met Marc Cohen on the ski slopes; he was her instructor. She soon became enthralled with the young Swiss mountain man. Marc could ski all day, looking so grand, legs pumping up and down so smooth, even on the moguls; and he could dance all night. Especially when the band at the chalet played new world ragtime. He took her in his arms dancing and she felt a sensuality that she never knew was a part of her. She wanted to stay in his powerful arms.

At seventeen she was captivated by the Swiss skier. He awakened a sexual side of her, suppressed deep within her being. She was in love for the first time. He was so romantic, bought her flowers and

Swiss chocolates. When he kissed her, he stole her breath away. She happily gave him all of her.

***

Marc was smitten by Katherine's beauty, her long brown hair bouncing when she skied or danced, her deep dark eyes pulling him into her soul. With her long legs and the curves of her hips and breasts his eyes couldn't escape her loveliness. She represented everything he was not—nobility. He was in love with her and unable to get enough of the girl.

***

Katherine brought him home. Her parents hated the "Swiss Italian Jew" as they secretly called him. They knew he was wealthy and ambitious, but he was new money and they were old wealth; landed Austrian nobility. They didn't want to lose their daughter to this foreigner. They had already suffered the loss and death of their son in the Great War.

Baron and Lady Wineheim hoped their daughter was just going through a phase, but Kathrine had discovered a powerful adolescent rebellion.

One weekend, she came back with a gaudy big diamond ring on her finger. They had eloped and her parents had to reluctantly accept Marc into their family. Soon Katherine realized she was pregnant.

Within a year her parents were gone, taken by the Spanish Flu. When Marc went back to work, she felt abandoned, staying in Austria, feeling fat, pregnant and alone. Where had the romance gone, she wondered?

***

Rose was the brave twin; she came out of the womb first. As they grew she showed a curious nature and had to beat her sister Iris in any game they played. Rose skied from the top of Mount Zermatt while Iris was still on the intermediate slopes. Rose gravitated towards her athletic father; she was Daddy's girl. Not that Marc didn't show love to Iris, but Rose's personality just clicked with her Dad's and the two became inseparable.

***

Katherine felt Marc had changed. Money became more important than she was. He spent all his time with his Italian and American bootleggers in Italy or off skiing every mountain in the Alps with Rose. Fights between Katherine and Marc became more and more heated. Rose sided with her father while Iris sided with her mother.

***

Rose enjoyed the company of her father's outlaws and started keeping his business books. She rebelled against her mother's old stodgy nobility. When the divorce came Katherine kept her family's estate. Marc Cohen kept control of his shipping interests. Katherine didn't want any of his ambitious new money. She got Iris, and he got Rose in the settlement.

Chapter 6

Summer-Autumn 1939

After devouring Austria, Germany gobbled up territory like hungry wolves let loose on a rabbit farm.

Hitler made a deal with Britain and France to take over the heavily guarded Sudetenland of Czechoslovakia. Shortly afterwards, the wolf pack gobbled up the rest of that small, proud country.

The Prime Minister of Britain, Neville Chamberlain, after ceding the Czech parcel to Hitler, came back to his island country with a treaty that he said would "give us peace in our time."

On September 1st Germany invaded Poland. Britain and France reluctantly entered the war.

***

Rose caught up with her father at their home in Zurich. Autumn leaves fell off trees like tears of Jewish mothers worried about their children under the Nazi regime.

“We have saved a hundred and fifteen Jews out of Austria while the Nazis arrested and relocated thousands,” Marc complained to Rose, a cigarette hanging from his lips. He smoked like Bogart; Marc Cohen always had a pack of Camels.

The Cohens for the most part saved families Iris and Rose knew from school, that they were able to get out with forged papers from Marc’s Mafioso friends. The Jewish families simply boarded trains through Switzerland and over the hump to Italy. And as everyone said, “the one good thing Mussolini did was get the trains to run on time.”

Then they boarded one of Marc's ships and were taken to Havana until they could be safely smuggled into the States.

"It seems futile but at least we saved a hundred and fifteen of our friends and neighbors."

Rose said, "Now that the war has spread to Poland, I don't know what to do, we knew Austrians that needed to get out but neither of us speak Polish."

"Dad, I think I'm going to try and get in touch with French Jews while that country is still free. The French and the English have more tanks than the Germans and hopefully the Maginot Line will keep the wolves away. But I have a feeling the French are sheep ready to be shorn."

Marc said, "Austria was one thing but I worry about you going to France, you don't have the contacts."

"I'd say it's time I make some," Rose replied.

Chapter 7

1939 - 1940

Poland fell to the Germans in two short months, with the Nazis using aircraft, tanks and infantry, decimating the under equipped Polish army. The Germans called their new tactics blitzkrieg or lightning war.

Next, they turned their blitz on the Belgians and then drove into France, circumventing the Maginot Line. It didn't take the German military machine long to have the French and British army in full retreat. France fell like a pine tree attacked with a chainsaw; only the miracle at Dunkirk saved the small British army and air corps to face the Huns alone.

***

Rose had always thought of France as a country full of color, with an array of flowers in window pots and women wearing rainbows of colorful clothing.

She couldn't help but notice the rainbows had been hidden away. Even rouge and lipstick were absent from female faces.

Rose encountered the two men that would change her life on the same day in occupied France. After meeting a promising resistance contact, Rose sat alone in an outdoor cafe in Nancy.

The first of the men was Captain Ramstein, a twenty-five-year-old Austrian, assigned to General Rommel's command. She thought he had movie star good looks with deep blue eyes, but Rose ignored the soldier. She couldn't see past the swastika on his shirt and hat.

The second was Corporal Frank Schmidt of the Gestapo, who looked like what he was, barbaric.

The corporal waved for Rose to sit with him. She declined, speaking only in French and quickly got up to leave.

He said to her in German, "What's the matter, Frenchy, you think you're too good for me?"

The Captain came to her rescue. "Corporal, leave the young lady alone."

Schmidt said, "Regular army should not mess with Gestapo."

Ramstein said, "I work for Rommel not for the Gestapo."

They both turned back to the girl but she had already disappeared.

Chapter 8

1940

Right in the middle of Europe, sitting above the fray of war, Switzerland proved to be a unique country. Without its own language, in areas near different surrounding countries, the Swiss spoke either French, Italian, German or even a Slavic derivative of speech. They had been able to stay neutral during the First World War and so far, their neutrality had been respected by the Axis powers despite being surrounded by the Fascists.

Why had Hitler allowed the Swiss neutrality, while his army invaded other neutral countries? One reason was their independent banking system that availed itself to the Germans. The second reason was the German general staff knew the Swiss were heavily armed and a blitzkrieg would be difficult to sustain through the mountain passes of the Alps. Any invasion could have dire consequences.

The Swiss found themselves in a sea of hostile forces and had to make some sacrifices to retain neutrality. Germany demanded control of trains going through Switzerland to Italy. Jews were not allowed to migrate to Switzerland. Yet if Jews found their way across the border the Swiss kept them in their own relocation camps rather than return them to the Nazis.

***

Rose made contacts with the new French underground but she had to be careful not to jeopardize Swiss neutrality. So, when in France she always wore a red wig and glasses and spoke only French. She had very good French identification papers, thanks to her father.

She was leading a family of Jews across the border when they were spotted by a group of Gestapo, led by the newly promoted Sargent Schmidt. The Germans swarmed up towards Rose's group. If she could get the family over the mountain pass, they would be safely in Swiss territory. She pointed to the short way across the border and split up with them hoping that the soldiers would come after her.

The ruse worked and Rose, dressed all in white, ducked under a snowy cornice and became invisible. The soldiers looked for her for a couple of hours as the sun beat down, her own sweat stinging her eyes. She couldn't move a muscle or she would give herself away.

Frustrated with losing his prey, Sargent Schmidt said, "What is she, a white fox? Damn her!"

Finally, in late afternoon the Germans gave up and marched away. Rose reached into her knapsack, pulled out small snowshoes and was over the border in minutes.

She met the family at the Swiss relocation center. She would not be able to get them to Italy but they were safely under Swiss protection.

Chapter 9

Autumn 1940

German military power appeared unstoppable. Almost the entire European continent had fallen under the Nazi jackboots. Only the Island of Britain was left to bear the brunt of the pain.

***

Rose sat sipping coffee in the same outdoor café in Nancy, France. The weather was unseasonably warm yet the streets, shops, and cafes were unusually empty. Even the birds muted their songs.

Captain Ramstein leaned over from the table behind her and said, "Mademoiselle, you are making a big mistake."

"I think what would be a big mistake would be talking to you," Rose said leaning away from him.

He scooted closer. "Me? No, I'm harmless. It is Gestapo Sargent Frank Schmidt you have to worry about seeing you here."

"I can tell, in spite of your best efforts to look indifferent, I have gained your attention."

"Why would Sargent Schmidt and the Gestapo be interested in me?" questioned Rose.

Captain Karl Ramstein said, "He believes you are the White Fox."

"What in the world is the White Fox?"

"It's the code name the Gestapo has given a young lady who is helping Jews get out of France. Listen we can't talk here, he could be along any minute. Quickly, come with me."

Rose asked, "Why should I come with you?"

"It's me or him, trust your instincts."

Rose weighed what she knew about the two men and followed her gut reaction. Schmidt was more dangerous to her than Ramstein.

"Okay, I'll follow you."

He led her to the movie theater a few blocks away, bought her a ticket and pointed her to a dark corner away from curious eyes.

"Why would a German soldier on Rommel's staff want to help me?" She asked him.

"Oh, so you do remember me."

"Yes," she said reluctantly. "But please answer my question."

"Let's just say, I think you're beautiful."

"I should slap you for that answer," she said, pushing him away.

"Why? I'm being nice and honest. Not all Germans are bad guys."

"Yeah, tell a Jew that," she said indignantly.

He said, “I have nothing against the Jews. I’m just a soldier trying to stay alive and to tell you the truth, I’m looking for romance.”

“Romance, no chance, you are looking in the wrong place.”

He said, “Would it help if I tell you I can not stand the Gestapo, for what they do and what they stand for.”

“Why do you hate them?”

“My best friend in college was Jewish and his sister was like…a sister to me.”

“That was a good answer,” she acknowledged.

“So, you will go out with me?” He asked.

Dramatic music came from the screen as Katherine Hepburn kissed Spencer Tracy.

“Meet me here next Friday, at 1300,” Rose said.

She walked away, disappearing into the darkened theater.

.

Chapter 10

1940

Bombs rained down on London night after night. Both the rich and the poor huddled in masses on subway platforms for protection.

Up in the darkened sky, hundreds of aircraft engaged in dogfights as they peaked in and out of searchlights.

Somehow the British pilots held their own against the much larger numbers of German fighters and bombers. As Winston Churchill declared "Never in the course of human events have so many owed so much to so few."

***

"So, Dad what do you think?" Rose asked, as they sat across from each other. The smell of garlic filled the noisy restaurant in Naples while they waited for their pizza.

"I don't like the chances you are taking. This Gestapo Sargent Schmidt sounds like a real piece of work. He won't stop until you are caught and I hate to think what he would do with you if that happens," Marc said blowing out a puff of smoke.

They were quiet for a moment as the waitress set down the pie. Each grabbed a piece with two hands not allowing the cheese to drip off.

"I know the Gestapo ranks are filled with sadistic half-humans. I'm asking you about Captain Karl Ramstein, do you think I should trust him?" She said between bites.

"Why would you take that chance?" Her father asked.

"I don't know. Something tells me he will be important to me and my work," Rose replied.

"I know that he is right, not all Germans are evil but most have been brainwashed by Nazi propaganda. I believe that if it came down to a choice to save himself or you, he would not save you."

Marc let that sink in a moment as he took a swig of beer.

Then he said, "Rose, I think you should end your trips into France and quit testing your luck."

"Sorry, I just can't do that. It's too important," Rose insisted.

"I knew you were going to say that." Marc took a deep breath and shook his head in sadness. "I raised you to be tough. You have been around gangsters for much of your life. Most of them I wouldn't trust as far as I could throw them. But others like Meyer Lansky, their word was golden. Be very careful who you choose to trust Rose. You are the flower with the thorns. Use all your assets, your beauty, your intellect, and your toughness. What did they call you? The White Fox?"

"Yes," she said, "isn't that a kick?"

"Yeah, I guess so. But damn it! Stay alive. I love you too much to lose you."

Chapter 11

January 1941

The Nazi invasion of England had been called off by the Germans. Against overwhelming odds, the British air forces turned back the much larger Luftwaffe. Without greatly superior air cover, the chances of success of an invasion seemed minimal to Hitler's High Command.

Disappointed but resigned, the Fuhrer cast his eye on a bigger prize. He was about to make the same grave mistake as Napoleon and invade the vast expanses of Russia.

***

When Rose showed up at the movie theater Captain Ramstein was waiting for her.

"You look lovely," he said, in broken French.

"Thank you." Rose wore a long green pleated skirt, a red blouse, black coat, with black beret over her red wig.

Karl's brown eyes sparkled and he smiled at the sight of the pretty young woman.

He said, "I've got your ticket. Shall we?"

They entered the theater and moved to an empty corner so they could converse by themselves.

The two had to lean together to hear each other over the sound of the gangsters on the screen.

"I'm so glad you came," Karl said, offering her a cigarette.

She shook her head. "I still don't trust you."

"I have a present for you Miss White Fox."

"Please no presents," she said.

"You will like this. It's not something you carry, it's information. The German army is shifting troops East."

"East, towards the Soviets? Why in the world would you tell me this?"

"I want you to trust me. I believe Hitler is going to destroy Germany. The faster we lose the war, the more of us will survive."

So, you are willing to be a traitor against the Nazis?"

"You still don't get me. I believe Hitler is the traitor. By the way do you speak English? French is my third best language," Karl said.

"Yes, I speak English."

"Thank God," he said in good American accented English.

Rose asked him, "How did you learn English?"

"Remember my Jewish classmate? We were at Princeton University," he said.

"In America?" She asked.

"New Jersey the last time I checked."

"How in the world did you get in the German Army?"

The Depression still had a grip on the U.S. so, I came back home to Berlin and I got drafted."

"How do I know you are not a double agent?" She asked.

"I could have turned you in already, but remember the last time we were together, I told you to check your gut. What is it telling you now?"

Without warning, he leaned forward and kissed her.

Surprising herself, she kissed him back.

So much for checking my gut, she thought.

After leaving Karl in the theatre, Rose quickly got in touch with her British connection and told him about the troop movements.

Chapter 12

1935 to February 1941

The seeds of the thorn-bush that would eventually grow into World War II were planted in 1935 when Mussolini's Italian Army invaded Ethiopia in Northeast Africa. Mussolini believed himself a modern-day Caesar. He needed an Empire. This new Roman Emperor almost bit off more than he could chew. Ethiopian King Haile Selassie's out-gunned warriors put up quite a struggle, holding out for over a year.

After Italy joined Germany in the Second World War, the British in 1940, with forces in Egypt, attacked the Italians in North Africa, sending them on a full inglorious retreat.

***

At their established meeting place at the movie theater, Karl told Rose the bad news, "Rommel is being assigned to North Africa so I must leave you."

Rose felt a tear roll down her face, surprised at her own strong reaction. After all she barely knew the young soldier.

He said, "I will miss seeing you more than you know. I was so attracted to your physical beauty and I must confess I love looking at you. But as I started to get to know you, I realized you are very special, brave, kind and totally lovable."

"You are quickly becoming special to me also." She grabbed the cigarette he was smoking, took a puff and handed it back. It bought her a smile.

Karl said, "Maybe you do like me a little."

"Captain Ramstein," Rose said, "I would like one last kiss to remember you by."

They fell into each other's arms and kissed long and hard yet tenderly. She felt her passion rise, as the hair on the back of her head tingled.

He whispered in her ear, "I've never felt like this with any woman before you."

He pushed her to arms length so he could look once deeply into her eyes. "Please remember me."

The lights came up. The movie was over.

Chapter 13

Summer 1941

After amassing its army in Poland, Germany invaded the USSR, breaking its treaty with the Communist country by driving overwhelming blitzes in numbers never seen before in warfare. The Russians fought and retreated much like they did before Napoleon's Grand Army. This time the enemy drove them back faster, to the gates of Leningrad and Stalingrad where staggering numbers of soldiers from each side went to die.

***

Working in France, Rose felt the Gestapo, SS and other Nazi's closing in. They raided trains; captured and tortured French underground members all over the countryside. Nowhere was safe. Jews were rounded up in ever greater numbers and were shipped East to points unknown.

She dyed her hair dark brown and cut it short but felt no safety with her disguise. It was getting harder and more dangerous to get Jews across the border. Only her knowledge of mountain passes allowed the last few escapes.

On a July evening, Rose drove a group of five Jewish freedom seekers on a mud and snow-covered mountain road. Suddenly, a French border patrol car appeared behind her and hit its siren. Lights flashing it chased after them. Rose accelerated and the race was on.

Around a narrow curve the patrol car slid into an embankment. Temporally ahead and out of their sight, she tucked her Citroen into a cave she knew hoping they wouldn't be found. The patrollers didn't see the cave opening and drove on past. She waited until the patrol car passed her coming back in the other direction.

Rose thought, first it was the Germans, then the Austrians, and now the French were all out to get her. Once safely across the border she decided she needed a break.

Chapter 14

1938 to December 1941

Katherine and Iris arrived in the United States as the Depression waned. People found jobs in the military buildup, as America became the arsenal of democracy even before it became a country at war. Tanks, planes and guns were beginning to come off the assembly lines, creating even more job opportunities.

Another employment avenue came with the end of prohibition. The Beer industry made St.Louis, with its location in the middle of the United States, a strategic place to distribute its product.

Katherine purchased farmland to grow hops and grain to produce beer. She also commissioned to have a grand house built on land that would become suburban Middletown, Missouri after the war.

She invested in a run-down old pre-prohibition beer brewery in St. Louis that would grow to be among the most successful in the United States.

Katherine thought it ironic that she was going into the same industry as her ex-husband, but unlike Marc, her brewery was completely legal and domestic as opposed to his involvement as a bootlegger during prohibition.

***

Iris attended high school in 1938, and went on to college at Columbia in New York as the second World War started. In late 1940 she began to date a Jewish boy, named Len Kleinman.

A native New Yorker, Len introduced Iris to the swinging night life of the country's largest city. Benny Goodman was a favorite of theirs and on a date the two college students danced to his big band 'till the early morning hours.

On a humid sweaty August night, they moved to the cool jazzy rhythms of Cab Calloway at the Cotton Club in Harlem where they kissed for the very first time. Iris felt herself deeply drawn to Len. Maybe because of her parent's unique divorce arrangements, she desperately missed male attention.

Whatever the reason she was falling hard for the young man; so different from the boys she dated back in Austria. He was so cool, so sophisticated, so good-looking; so American.

Walking back to campus after the nightclub, they lingered over passionate kisses. Len pulled out a ring and asked, "Will you marry me?"

"Oh yes, yes," she said, planting a big kiss on his neck, smearing her lipstick, leaving raspberry red stains on his white collar.

They decided to check into the Waldorf to celebrate and made love until the sun came up.

"Hope it didn't hurt," he asked afterwards as they lay together, passion spent. "Are you okay?"

"Yes, yes, yes, hell yes!" She said laughing, punctuating with a kiss after each affirmative answer.

"That was great for our first time. I think we'll get much better with practice," he said, tickling her.

Len smiled looking at Iris, "God, I'm so happy, I feel like I could burst. You are the most beautiful girl in the whole wide world."

Iris thought of her sister and said, "Maybe, maybe not."

"What do to mean by that?" He asked.

She said, "Let me tell you about my twin sister Rose…"

***

Iris and Len were lounging on the bed on December 7th, 1941 studying for a test together when an announcement came on the radio:

THIS MORNING THE JAPANESE

IMPERIAL FLEET WITHOUT

PROVOCATION ATTACKED

PEARL HARBOR IN HAWAII

PRESIDENT FRANKLIN D.

ROOSEVELT HAS ASKED

CONGRESS FOR A

DECLARATION OF WAR

***

"Holy shit!" Len said, "This changes everything. School is suddenly not so important. I feel compelled to do my part. I guess I'll be joining up soon."

"You can't just go and leave me all alone."

"We'll get married before I go, alright?"

"I know you have to go but damn it, stay out of trouble."

The next week Germany declared war on the United States.

A month later, after Iris and Len were married at City Hall, Len joined the Army Air Corp.

Chapter 15

February – April 1942

As the United States entered the war, facing overwhelming defeat at Pearl Harbor, the country took stock in how unprepared it was. To fight a full-scale war against the might of the Japanese in the Pacific and the German military machine in Europe and North Africa there was much to be done.

One bit of good news from the fiasco in Hawaii; three Aircraft Carriers were not in port during that fateful day and became available to mount attacks against a superior Japanese Naval Force.

German submarines attacked and sank American transports off the Atlantic coast while convoys were being desperately organized.

The Japanese overran American forces in the Philippines and MacArthur retreated to Australia.

Helping American morale, the Doolittle raid was launched from the Carrier Hornet while special long range B29's successfully attacked Tokyo.

***

With the United States in the war after Pearl Harbor, Marc Cohen moved his maritime American liquor export business headquarters out of Italy to London. His ships drafted, with his permission, to carry food and munitions desperately needed in England.

Rose and her Dad retreated to their modest but comfortable home outside of Zurich after her traumatic car chase avoiding the French Border Patrol. Sitting with her father over a dinner of her favorite comfort food, sausage and sauerkraut, they discussed Rose's future.

Marc said, “It’s time you started your formal college education. I’d like you to move to London with me. With your smarts and my money, I’m sure we can get you into a good school.”

Rose said, “With all the bombing going on in London, I’m not sure it would be much of a break from the dangerous things I was doing in France.”

Marc said, “It doesn’t have to be in London, I hear there are very good schools at Oxford and Cambridge.”

“That sounds like a good idea Dad, I’ll apply to both of them and see if I get accepted.”

Rose easily got into Oxford, taking the long and dangerous boat ride from Naples to England.

She read about the London blitz. Arriving at the English capital, she was amazed at all the damage done by the Nazi bombings, especially in the seaport industrial area. Whole blocks were destroyed, with crowds of people walking aimlessly or lying homeless in the streets. The whole scene left her depressed but even more determined to make a difference.

***

At Oxford, she could temporarily leave the war behind and imagine seeing Alice chase the rabbit to the Mad Hatter's party at the school where Lewis Carroll wrote the classic children's story. She applied herself to regular lower division classes and enjoyed a diversity of learning.

One foggy morning, as she was walking across campus, her math professor, Dr. Sutterhand intercepted her.

"It has come to my attention that you were working with the French underground."

Rose said, "Whatever in the world gave you that idea?"

He said, “It is my job to know these kinds of things. I am with the British Intelligence Service. I would like to offer you a job.”

“I came here to get a more formal education.”

The professor said, “It doesn’t have to be one or the other, you can get college credit while working with us.”

“I need to take some time to think about this, all right?”

“Of course,” Dr. Sutterhand said, “but don’t take too much time; the war is going to go on with or without you, and I’m hoping it will be *with* you”. He smiled confidently, turned and walked away.

Chapter 16

June - October 1942.

General Rommel with Karl Ramstein at his side, out thought and out maneuvered his British rivals in North Africa so intently that he gained the nickname "The Desert Fox." He chased the English back to Egypt and overran the stronghold of Tobruk in spite of Churchill's assurances that it couldn't be taken.

***

Rose weighed the pros and cons of Dr. Sutterhand's offer and felt she was ready to get back in the fight.

She accepted her professor's invitation to join British Intelligence and immediately felt like a hundred-pound weight had been taken off her shoulders. She was no longer fighting a private war, trying to decide who to save and who had to be left to the wolves.

Rose became part of a team. The English immersed her in an intense underground boot-camp program that included, self-defense exercises, training with all types of weapons and hand to hand combat.

Skiing already had her in good shape but this new exercise regime was beyond any physical workouts she had ever experienced. Rose's body became hard, toned, muscled. She ran miles and swam in frigid sea-water.

Each night her body was painfully sore but her confidence skyrocketed. She held her own against powerful men almost twice her weight.

Besides her training program, Rose went to work for the Navy Department. With her experience at fleet organization for her father, the Admiralty used her talents to help organize convoys. Something the

English desperately needed. The German packs of submarines were reeking havoc on Allied shipping.

She also took classes with naval officers about war and intelligence strategy.

A young Ensign in her class, Roger Palmer, looked like Cary Grant and sounded like Laurence Olivier. He smelled of Bay Rum aftershave.

Palmer often met her for lunch, which soon led to dinner. They started dating. After going to a movie, the Ensign held her hand. Then came a goodnight kiss, which Rose rather enjoyed.

Roger took her back to his room after the next date and the couple started kissing. Rose allowed him to feel under her bra, while her hands roamed to his chest, their passion building. Rose thought about losing her virginity with Roger, but something didn't feel right. She found herself thinking of Karl Ramstein and wished she was with him.

She said, “Roger please stop. It’s too much too soon.”

“Sorry, I didn’t mean to take advantage,” Roger said.

“No, you have been…a gentleman…but I don’t want to lead you on. Maybe if we take things slower?”

“I can do that…whatever you are ready for.”

“Thank you. But I’m just not ready for this.”

Roger said, “I was falling in love with you. With the war on…you know. It’s hard to go slow, death could call at any time. Would you feel better if we got married?” Rose saw the disappointment and sadness on his face. She felt sorry to have caused it.

But she said, “Oh Roger, no. I like you but no. I think I might be in love with someone else.”

And damn it! He is wearing the wrong uniform.

Chapter 17

November 8,1942

Casablanca, French North Africa

The Allied invasion of French (Vichy) North Africa started with a cannonade from warships lined up in the Mediterranean as far as the Vichy French defenders could see. Explosion after explosion came from the big guns of the Allied fleet.

Following the naval bombardment came an overwhelming invasion force that landed on the beaches. An army of French underground, over four-hundred strong, joined the attack and after light resistance the Allied forces took the city of Casablanca.

At the same time from the other side of North Africa, in Egypt, British General Montgomery attacked

Rommel's German forces. The Desert Fox's North Africa Corp found themselves fighting to hold off Allied attacks from two sides.

***.

Len Cohen loved flying. On the early morning of November 8, 1942, his bomber squadron took off from Gibraltar, making the long run across the Mediterranean Sea, to drop ordnance on the enemy at Casablanca in support of Operation Torch.

On his final bombing run, one of the engines of his B17 took a hit from flack. He had no choice but to put the aircraft down. He made a perfect landing on the enemy's runway. His crew surrendered to the French but they would set the World War II record for the shortest time as POWs; minutes later the French garrison surrendered to the Americans.

***

That same morning Rose watched the bombardment of Casablanca from the sea, awed by its ferocity. She had been assigned to a British cruiser on that bright clear morning, watched the bombardment from the bridge and was assigned to go ashore and translate if needed.

Rose stepped off the ship and ran into an American flyer who was being told in French, he was no longer a prisoner. She translated this circumstance into English for him and introduced herself as Rose Cohen.

She was met with an opened mouth stare from the brown eyed pilot.

"Do you have a sister?" He asked awkwardly.

"Yes. Why do you ask?"

"Cause I'm married to a woman who looks exactly like you."

"You must be Len."

"Yes," he said. "How in the world…?" He laughed as the answer came to him. "Of course, your Rose."

Rose smiled her sweetest smile and misquoting Bogart in the then popular new movie, *Casablanca* said, "Of all the battles in the world you had to fall into mine."

He laughed and said, also misquoting the movie, "Rose, this just may be the beginning of a great friendship."

After getting permission from their superiors, the brother and sister in-law went off to a French restaurant for lunch. The couldn't find *Rick's Café*, so they settled for a little French-African Bistro.

Rose said, "I hope you don't mind if I order. I'm quite used to French food."

Len said, "Have at it. It's so strange having lunch with you. I almost feel like I'm with my wife."

"It kind of reminds me of some dates my sister and I had when we switched places," she said laughing.

"The tale of this chance meeting would make a great letter to Iris, but who knows what would be left after the censors got through with it," Rose mused.

"I'll write to her tonight as I do most nights. I'll tell her I met a perfect Rose. But as Shakespeare said, "Would a Rose by the name of Iris smell as sweet? Or something like that."

"Just don't let the censors know where you found the Rose and it might work."

Lunch was superb. They started with a cucumber salad followed by split lamb and shrimp kabobs reeking of garlic with couscous as a side dish and shared a bottle of blood red Bordeaux through the meal.

Rose glanced at Len, the cute curly brown-haired Jew from New York City and wondered what it was like to be married to him, going to Broadway plays, dancing until dawn to jazz bands in Harlem. She lived a little vicariously through Iris.

The waiter brought the coup-de-grace, a pastry filled with rich chocolate cream for dessert. It would be the best meal that either would have for a while.

Chapter 18

June 1943

With the surrender of the French in North Africa the Germans in France moved in to occupy Vichy, the "Free" half of France. In just days, the maps of Western Europe and North African changed radically.

***

Upon returning from her North Africa trip, Rose walked in to MI6 headquarters at Oxford. Professor Shutterhand told her, "Rose we have an essential job for you. A group of resistance fighters need to get out of Vichy, France."

"You will night parachute in, meet the fighters outside Leon and take them over the mountains, then sneak them into Switzerland."

"Great," she said, with full sarcasm "You are starting me with something easy. If I don't break my leg on the dangerous night jump, or get caught, I lead a group of strangers over a major mountain range and deliver them past the Swiss Border Guards to the British Embassy. Right?"

"That's about it. Nothing you can't handle, right?" The professor said with a totally straight face.

We've got you new passports and papers, the last name of Cohen we believed sounded too Jewish to get past the Germans."

"So, what's my new name?"

"It's Rose Zorra, that is Spanish for a female fox," Sutterhand said. We believe a Spanish name would be remote enough to get by, with French and German the major languages you will be dealing with. Zorro was a major hero in Mexican-California before it broke away from Spain. Zorra will be your code name.

Rose said, “Sounds good to me but I could sure use a few days off.”

“Sorry, would it help if I told you the mission is very important?”

“Okay,” she said sarcastically with a phony smile, “I’m in as long as it’s important. What about my disguise?”

He said, “We cut your hair short, dye it black and give you big ugly glasses.”

“Really, that’s the best you could come up with?”

The Professor just shrugged his shoulders.

She laughed, “Well ugly glasses work for Superman in the comic books. Maybe it will work for me.”

***

The night of the jump there was no moon and a clear sky. The pilot announced, "Five minutes, Miss. Zorra."

Rose checked her watch, hooked up and was guided out the door for her first jump into hostile territory. The ground came up almost too fast but like in practice when her feet hit the ground, she rolled into a perfect landing. She gathered her chute and hid it under the deep rich smelling forest mulch. Thanks, she said silently to the white silk, which was no longer needed.

She stripped off the jump suit and added it to the parachute. Her pack provided the skirt and blouse of a French girl. Rose checked her map and compass with her torch and was off to the hideout, a solitary cabin in the woods. So far so good.

Before dawn she arrived, and met the seven escapees, six men and one young woman as Rose had been told.

Rose instructed them to pair off, after showing on the map where to meet at the end of the forest trail. She took the nervous girl under her wing and with a pat on the shoulder said, “Let’s go.”

Talking was discouraged. The less they knew about each other the better, in case anyone was caught.

Miraculously they never encountered any authorities along the way. It seemed everyone was laying low as the Nazis moved into Vichy. The eight of them reconnoitered at the end of the trail.

Rose's expertise about climbing in the Alps was desperately needed. She guided them off the trail and they started up the mountain, Rose leading the way.

Higher they went, traversing a shear wall of rock and snow, but Rose’s confidence was contagious and they slowly worked their way up.

Without warning a squad of Nazi soldiers appeared below them and were climbing quickly towards them. Rose told her group, “Keep along the right side of the rock face. Look forward not back, I'll take care of them and catch up with you."

Rose shimmied up a snow bank, took out a hand grenade and tossed it to the heavy snow ledge below her. The explosion blew a hole in the snow and the ice ridge collapsed just below her feet.

It started an avalanche. A wall of white toppled slowly at first, then it picked up speed and spilled down the ridge. As if by magic the pursuers were gone, wiped off the mountain. It was an old trick she learned, out with her friends in the ski patrol.

Rose caught up with the group and by nightfall they reached the top, safely in Switzerland. Coming off the mountain, they simply caught a train to Bern.

When the doors opened the next morning in the capital, all eight of the resistance fighters piled into the British Embassy.

Rose was amazed. It all seemed too easy. Somehow, she made the outrageous plan run like a Swiss time-piece.

Chapter 19

July 1943

U.S. Aircraft attacked Hamburg, Germany in the largest bombing raid of the war up to that point. Rome was bombed for the first time. Patton captured Palermo, Sicily.

***

The young woman that Rose escorted to safety was on the same plane to London. They sat together and found they had things in common.

Rose said, "Your English and your French are really good, where are you from?"

The girl answered, "My father is English and my mother is French, my older brother and I went back and forth between the two countries."

"I don't even know your name," Rose said.

"Lily, my name is Lily Atwood."

Rose laughed, "That is so funny, my name is Rose and I have a twin sister named Iris. You would fit right in with the flower family."

Lily turned toward her. Rose thought she was pretty with dark hair, sparkling brown eyes. Her face crinkled when she laughed.

"How old are you?" Rose asked.

"I'm twenty-one."

She was rather thin and small breasted, making her look younger than her twenty-one years.

'How old are you?" Lily asked.

“I’m twenty-one also.”

“That seems impossible! I thought you were much older than me, especially when you led us up that mountain.”

“Well, I’m Swiss, I grew up in those mountains,” Rose replied.

Lily said, ‘Swiss, that explains your knowledge of languages.”

Rose said, “Yeah, I naturally speak French, German, Italian and of course English. Most Swiss speak English.”

“You probably have one of those Swiss Army knives in your pocket.”

Rose laughed and said, “Yeah, I can open a bottle of wine while I’m killing somebody, those things come in quite handy in times of war—and peace.”

They giggled. Lily said, "I thought the Swiss were supposed to be neutral."

Rose added, "I'm also one quarter Jewish."

Lily frowned. "Okay I get it now."

Rose said, "I miss my sister, she's off living in America. I hope we can become friends Lily, I need a friend."

***

Back in Oxford, they went to a jazz club and danced all night with different American men. Taking a break sitting at a side table sipping some ale, Rose said, "You know what they say about all the American boys in England? *They are over-sexed, over-paid and over here,* but I sure like them." The two girls laughed.

They excused themselves and sauntered off to the bathroom together. Rose saw a weird tattoo on Lily's leg but chose not to say anything about it.

Chapter 20

August to October 1943

George Patton proved to be the most capable strategist of the American generals, keeping Rommel on the run in North Africa then leading the charge and conquering Sicily.

After Sicily the natural target was Mussolini's Italy. However, that would prove to be a much harder olive to swallow.

The United States forces attacked the toe of the Italian boot. With the arrival of an American army on their mainland the Italian military in Southern Italy surrendered to the Yanks.

Mussolini found himself overthrown by the High Command of the Italian army and arrested; but the Germans raided the jail and freed the Italian dictator.

When the Allies attacked in Italy, they were too late. The Germans had moved masses of troops down the peninsula and controlled the mountainous high ground.

With Mussolini relegated to a figurehead, the fighting in Italy became a confused slugfest. The Italian Army, not knowing who to follow, broke up into gangs for control of their own neighborhoods.

***

After her foray in North Africa, Rose returned to MI6's headquarters in Oxford.

"Miss. Zorra, there is a radio call for you from a Marc Cohen. He says it's important," a young Lieutenant said.

"Dad, where are you?"

"At our ski cabin in Northern Italy. Listen, things have totally gone to shit here, with fascists hunting anti-fascists. Even Jews that Mussolini left alone are being rounded up. There are many of us hiding in the mountains. Can you do your magic and come get us out?"

"Dad, give the instructions to this lieutenant. I'll see what I can do. And Dad, collect all the white sheets you can find."

"Rose, I don't want to surrender."

Rose laughed, "Not for surrender, we'll use them for camouflage. I'll get there as soon as I can."

***

It took Rose three days to get to the cabin. British Intelligence (MI6)) wanted information from behind the German lines in Northern Italy and procured her a place on a DC10 transport. The plane had to circumnavigate from England to North Africa, to Sicily and finally up the Aegean Sea for the night drop in the foothills below the Italian Alps.

Hiking all night, she reached her father's cabin as the colors of dawn crested behind the late winter grandeur of the Matterhorn and Zermatt. Despite her exhaustion, she smiled. The mountains felt like home, where she and her dad skied so often.

Keeping watch, her father spotted her and dashed down the hill from the cabin to greet her, his arms opened. "How's my little soldier?"

"Tired," she said as she entered the warmth of his embrace.

"Come inside, have some porridge, while I explain our situation. Then you can get some sleep."

Rose entered the "cabin" which was actually a large house owned by her father's conglomerate. She had been there often on cross country ski trips. She noticed the place was overrun with people. They were scattered in sleeping bags laying all over the first floor.

She sat at the table, was handed a hearty bowl of oatmeal and a mug of some dark warm liquid.

Her father attempted to explain the confused situation. "The Italian countryside is a total mess. Mussolini is supposed to be back in power, but if not for the German occupation he would have been executed. He no longer has any real authority."

"Believe it or not the German SS and Gestapo are arresting anti-fascists and Jews, to be loaded onto trains headed to Eastern Europe for what we guess are slave labor camps. Sometimes if the Nazis aren't near the trains, they have the Jews dig pits and shoot them."

A look of disgust clouded his face. Rose noticed he looked much older than the last time they had been together.

"The Italian Fascists are hunting the underground army and communists, but most of the population can't tell who is who. The Italian army that surrendered and declared war against Germany when the Americans invaded has mostly headed for the hills. The whole country is screwed up."

"There are thirty-six of us, many of my workers and their families, Jewish families we know, and others who didn't know where to go."

Rose finished what little she had been given to eat and asked, "What weapons do we have?"

"Half of us have hunting rifles, we have two Thompsons. I have one and Charlie, my Executive Officer has the other. You remember Charlie, don't you?"

The man with the familiar face waved to Rose. She waved back trying to show him a smile.

Marc continued, "We also have twelve hand guns."

"Not much of an arsenal," Rose said, "were you able to get sheets?"

“We have about ten in the cabin.”

“That will have to do. Wake me in a few hours or if we are attacked,” she added.

Rose went up to her old room from her teen years, single bed, a now empty dresser. She fell into the bed and was out before she could turn the light switch off.

***

Two hours later, her father woke her. “They are coming.”

She forced herself awake. “I guess it’s showtime.”

The weather turned cold and clear. Rose wore her usual white down jacket, ski pants and white knit hat. Those that had them, covered themselves with white sheets as camouflage on the snow. Rose laughed, they looked like ghosts from pictures of American Halloween parties.

Only Rose and Marc knew the way over the mountain and through the pass to Switzerland. She led and he took up the rear. They hadn't gone more than fifty meters when a single shot rang out.

Red blood poured from the hole in Marc Cohen's head as he fell on the white snow.

"NO!" Rose screamed, her legs buckled and tears ran down her face. She wiped them away. "Buck up Rose," she shouted to herself. This is WAR. She had no time to stop and mourn or bury her father. Despite her feelings of horror, she had a job to do. Any grieving would have to wait.

Rose turned to her experience and training. People, families, looked to her to save them.

She flattened her body, stomach to the ground, aimed and fired. The man who had hit her father fell with a hole in his face, pouring crimson onto the icy snow. She took a second shot and another man fell.

She squeezed off three more shots hitting her targets. The enemy assault group quickly retreated.

Abandoning her father, Rose yelled to the rest of the group, "Follow me."

She wasn't about to let her father's death be in vain.

Rose had to lead this group of frightened people out of the darkness to safety. It took all her strength physically and mentally to get them over the mountains and she led them to a temporary promised land of safety, on Swiss soil.

They came off the mountain and boarded a train to Bern and turned themselves in at the refugee center.

At the British Embassy, Rose made her sad report and asked for a pick up. She was told by the Professor, "We have an easy job for you. You are to meet and pick up a double agent I believe you know, a German Major, Karl Ramstein."

Rose felt a warmth go through her cold body. Finally, something to look forward to. Only then she allowed herself to break down and cry for her father.

Chapter 21

May 1944

The Soviet Union turned back the Nazi offensive at Stalingrad but each side fought desperately for every mile during the German retreat from Russia.

General Eisenhower, appointed Supreme Commander in Europe, readied the Allied troops to invade occupied France. Patton's army, under Eisenhower's command was placed across from Calais to fool the Germans into expecting the invasion there. But Normandy was the chosen landing spot.

***

Rose sipped an espresso as she sat at a French cafe in Lyon. Clouds danced ominously in the sky looking like they might bring rain; unusual for this late in the spring. She arrived early for her meeting with Karl Ramstein, double agent and longtime target of her romantic crush. He claimed to have important information about Hitler's seawall.

She had daydreamed about this man for so long. What about him floated her boat? Was it his movie star good looks? His confidence? His ability to make her feel safe in unsafe places? Or had she just created a fantasy man to think about when she was alone and lonely? She wasn't sure but she had been unable to dispel his image from her mind the last two years.

Rose, so excited to see Karl, let her guard down.

***

Sargent Schmidt passed by. He saw Rose's face, the gorgeous face he couldn't get out of his mind. Could it really be the damn, White Fox? The fantasy of his evil dreams.

He snuck up behind her, put a gun to the back of her head and said, “Fraulein put your hands behind your back.” He snapped handcuffs on tight.

“Walk in front of me and don’t do anything unusual or I will blow your head off.”

He now had her total attention. As she walked, she looked for an out, but none appeared.

They entered what looked like an old abandoned house. In fact, it was his own private torture chamber.

“We are going to have some fun now, or should I say, I’m going to have some fun.”

He pulled off her shoes and stripped off her clothing piece by piece; ripping the shirt off her back, her bra, skirt and finally her underwear. She had a knife and a gun under her clothing. He lay her knife and gun behind him on the floor.

He laughed out loud. “Yes, I’m going to have some fun with you, my dear.”

He sat her in a chair totally naked, exposed, and pulled her arms back. He snapped the handcuffs behind her. His hands crudely stroked her body and roughly pinched the nipples of her breasts.

***

Rose figured he brought many a victim to this room. She had to keep her wits about her and she needed some luck.

She remained quiet, terrified but not showing him the satisfaction of fear.

"You are going to tell me all your contacts in the underground. Tell me when you are ready to talk."

She sat silently.

"Not yet, all right. Let's start with this."

He punched her face below her right eye, hitting her hard. It swelled and turned an ugly shade of black and blue.

He said, “Ready yet? No?” and let out a demonic laugh before he hit her again below her other eye making it hard to see his ugly face.

“Ready to talk yet? No?” He hit her in the gut. Vomit spew from her mouth and slopped onto the floor.

Sweat ran down her face.

“Ready yet?” He sang like a song out of tune.

He hit her nose. She felt it crack, her bright red blood ran down her naked chest like a small river between her breasts.

Rose realized, she was in for hours, days or weeks of torture that could only end with her death. She had to take a risk.

The wolf appeared to have all the power.

But the fox thought of a trick to play.

With the next punch, she threw herself backwards while tucking her head forward. The old wooden chair split open like an egg.

Before Schmidt could go for his gun, Rose's naked foot karate kicked his knee.

He went sprawling to the floor.

Rose jumped high, cat like and bent her legs, moving the handcuffs in front of her like Harry Houdini. She picked up a shattered chair leg.

Schmidt froze in panic.

She swung the wooden weapon as hard as she could, connecting with the Nazi's face.

Stunned, Schmidt dove for his gun.

Rose grabbed her knife off the floor and stabbed the Gestapo Sargent in the neck.

A new river of red joined her blood on the floor.

. One last time the chair leg smashed down on his head. She checked. Sargent Schmidt was dead.

Chapter 22

Late May 1944

The Allies in Italy linked up the troops fighting in Southern Italy with the ones that landed further up the boot at Anzio. They all turned north to capture Rome. The Germans retreated further and built a strong defensive line north of the capital.

***

With her clothing destroyed, Zorra took Schmidt's jacket off the hook, found his keys and unlocked the cuffs. She rubbed her raw wrists, belted her tormentors coat like a dress and went off to look for Karl.

Rain fell steadily, like the tears of relief.

Rose found him in the café. Karl took one look at her bloodied puffy face and held her in a tender embrace.

"What happened to you?" He asked.

"Sargent Schmidt," she answered.

"I'll kill him," Karl said.

"Too late. He's dead. I already killed the bastard," she said, tears running down her face.

"I'll get us a room somewhere quiet. Okay?"

She begged, "Get me off the street, hurry please."

The two attendants at the front desk did not question the German officer checking in with the girl with a swollen face; they looked down at their shoes and wondered, was it from him, or because of him.

In the room, he drew her a bath, applied cold towels to her face, oh so tenderly. "Does it hurt when I kiss you?" He asked, gently kissing her lips.

"Yes," she said, "but kiss me some more. "Don't you dare stop," she whispered breathlessly.

She kissed him back without fear. Passion overtaking her pain."

He showed her tenderness, kissing every spot that was not swollen or bruised.

Her hunger for him took over and she claimed control of lovemaking, mounting him; easing her pain.

After his seed filled her. She smiled, scratching her fingernails on his chest. She laughed out loud. She could no longer be called a maiden, and happily no longer a virgin.

"What is so funny?"

"I remember asking other girls if it hurt the first time. If I only knew."

"I'm so sorry. I tried to be careful," he said.

"No, you were great, I just didn't expect to get beaten up before making love the first time."

He kissed her behind the neck. "Did that hurt?" He asked.

"No. That felt good."

"Okay, that's my spot," he laughed and kissed that place over and over again.

"You have just one hour to stop that," she moaned. With passion building, they made love again.

***

Later, much later, satiated, showered and attacking a room service dinner, she asked Karl, "So, are you ready to defect? After my run in with your countryman, I'm anxious to get back to England,"

"I can't go yet, but I do have information. Rommel believes Patton will lead the invasion and come ashore at Calais."

"Good, that might help but why aren't you coming back with me?"

"I think I might be able to help Rommel keep his job after the invasion."

"Oh, Karl come back with me now, please."

"You still don't totally trust me?" He asked

"I'm here and I love you. But if you don't come back with me…I don't know if I can trust you."

"But after the landing, I may need to save Rommel. He is an honorable man. Please, no one can know what I've done."

"No damn it! Come with me now or I won't be able to forgive you," she said.

"You have to, I can't live without you, my love," he pleaded.

"Then come with me now, you do not owe anything to General Rommel, but if you stay, you may share his guilt. He is a Nazi."

"No, he's not. He is just a soldier fighting for his country."

"And who is his leader?"

Karl looked at her with pleading eyes.

"Who is his leader? Damn it! Karl. You must take off that uniform now, the one with the swastikas, and come with me or I'll never speak to you again. Karl, look at my face. Do you see what that Nazi did to me? Are you one of them? I am trying to save you from yourself. You have been playing both sides. It is time to choose. Are you really a member of the Third Reich? Or are you ready to join the fight against what they stand for?"

He looked at her. Her face swollen, two black eyes peering out at him. She was so brave and he loved her more than his love for his bedeviled country.

"Yes, of course you are right, I'll come with you."

***

The Double agent Karl Ramstein was required to be interviewed by MI6. Professor Sutterhand led the two-agent panel including British Military Officer, Captain Wilson.

"You have occasionally given us useful information as a member of General Rommel's staff. Why?" The Professor asked.

Ramstein answered, "Because I hate Hitler and everything he stands for."

Sutterhand said, "Despite that, you became a member of Rommel's staff. Explain that."

Ramstein said, "I didn't have a choice. I was drafted into the German army and wanted to stay alive. I respect General Rommel. I believe he is a good man just fighting for his country."

"I see you wanted it both ways," Wilson said.

"I want the Allies to win the war, and get rid of Hitler and his Nazis, so I can go back home to Berlin. Is that playing it both ways?" Ramstein said with a deep sigh. "The whole mess weighs deeply on my conscience."

"Why did you admire Rommel so much? You tried to help him win the war," the Professor challenged him.

"I confess, I did at times. I worked closely with the man for years. Let me tell you he is a great general, a great leader of men. He treated the Italians under his command the same as the Germans. He doesn't buy into all that superior race Hitler stuff."

Captain Wilson said, "I don't know if you deserve a medal or a firing squad."

Ramstein asked, "Do you want me to answer that?"

"Yes," Wilson said.

Karl answered, "I can remember reading English history. Just a few hundred years ago, Protestants were killing Catholics and Catholics were killing Protestants on your home island and look at the mess you made in Ireland. Your major allies, the Americans do not treat Negros well and of course what they did to the Indians could be called evil. Maybe all our hands are a little dirty."

Sutterhand said, "Thank you Major Ramstein. You are dismissed. We will get back to you."

The Professor turned to Rose who had been listening in behind a two-way mirror and asked her, "Do you trust this man?"

"I trust him with my life but maybe not with yours," she said.

"What do you suggest we do with him?" The Professor asked.

"Don't let him out of my sight," Rose suggested.

The two on the panel agreed. The Western Allies would need people like him to help put Germany back together after the war.

Chapter 23

June 5 – 6, 1944

The commanders of Operation Overlord, more popularly known as D-Day were huddled in the command headquarters in the south of England. They waited with great concern, for the deluge of rain to dissipate. Commander in Chief of the Allied Forces, Dwight D. Eisenhower met with his meteorologists and asked, "Do you think the rain will end by tomorrow?"

"It does not look good," the Senior Weather Specialist said, shaking his head.

A brave young weatherman said, "I think we will have a window."

"What does that mean?" The General asked.

"I think the weather will break tomorrow, sir."

"Who agrees?"

A majority of the weathermen held up their hands. Sweat stains showing on their underarms due to the pressure of the decision and the closeness of the men, in the warm humid room on the southern coast of England.

Eisenhower weighed the odds. The invasion was already a day behind. The ships were all loaded and ready to go. If they cancelled again, German intelligence could discover their plans and any chance of surprise may be lost. On the other hand, inclement weather with big waves bouncing and sinking landing craft would be a disaster.

Eisenhower said, "We Go."

June 6, 1944 would forever be known as D-Day, the allied invasion of France.

***

The morning of June 6, Rose and Ramstein found themselves assigned to the deck of a destroyer sending landing craft to Omaha Beach.

The landing beaches below Hitler's defensive seawall, built and defended by General Rommel became a killing zone, with heavy artillery. Machine gun nests kept Allied landing troops pinned down. Unable to move forward, the men were being cut to shreds.

Ramstein implored the destroyer's Captain to move in closer and he would direct him to the targets he emplaced while under Rommel's command.

"Aim your guns there, there and there," Karl pointed directly.

Quickly three artillery cannons were taken out of action by the destroyers' guns, opening a hole in the seawall for the allied soldiers to pour through. The battle turned.

Professor Sutterhand called Ramstein on the ship's radio.

"Major, that was impressive. I guess today, you will get a medal, not a firing squad."

***

For his part, General Rommel was absent. He looked at the weather and decided the invasion could not possibly come through the storm and went back home to visit his wife for her birthday.

Hitler went to sleep the evening of June, 5 and told his staff not to wake him. He also said not to release the reserve tanks without his permission. Even when Hitler awoke and the landing had taken place, he would not order in the reserves, believing Normandy was a faint and the main landings would be under Patton's command at Calais. The ruse of Patton's army across the channel from Calais worked perfectly.

***

Chapter 24

Late June - July, 1944.

Everywhere in the European theater of World War II the Germans were on the retreat. The Soviets regained the land they had lost in two years of the German Blitzkrieg.

In France the Allied invasion force made slow but steady progress despite slogging through the northern country hedgerows where Germans could hide and blast American made Sherman tanks with artillery from their powerful Panzer tanks.

***

Golder's Green, a middle-class enclave in North London became a center for Jewish refugees during the war. The smell of hot pastrami wafted through the air from the Kosher delicatessen down the block.

Assuming London was safe from enemy bombing, Rose moved her company headquarters to a house in that neighborhood. Both Rose and Karl made the deli a favorite place for lunch, where they would split a pastrami on rye bread, a potato knish and a big kosher dill pickle. Because she found herself the new CEO of Cohen Incorporated since the death of her father, Rose asked MI6 for a brief leave of absence to get her affairs in order.

***

Waking after a passionate night of love making, Rose felt morning kisses behind her neck working their way down her back. "You are insatiable!" She shouted.

Karl said, "I don't even know what that means. But if you said I can't get enough of you, that would be correct."

She turned to face him, a hungry smile on her face and returned the favor, kissing all over his body. He squirmed with pleasure.

It felt like they were trying to make up for all the time they were apart.

Finally, showered and dressed, Rose asked, "Do you love me?"

"What a silly question? Let's see, how did Shakespeare say it? 'I love you more than a summer's day,' or something like that."

Rose laughed. "Yeah, something like that, but no more poetry, I want a straight answer. Do you really love me?"

"Yes, Rose I love you."

"All right then let's get married," she proposed.

"Don't you think that might screw up your job as a spy? I might be a liability."

"My god, there is so much you don't know about me," she said.

"I could say the same about you. You know nothing about my family," he said.

"You're right, let's open up that can of worms," she said and reached across the table to hold his hand. "You go first."

"All right. You know I was born in Austria but my family is from Berlin."

"Yes of course."

"My father is a mechanical engineer. He works in northern Germany but even I don't know what he does. It's top-top-secret. My mother is back in Berlin. She was not allowed to travel with him. I had an older brother who was an officer in the Army, but he died at Stalingrad."

"I'm sorry for your loss," Rose said and squeezed his hand.

"I guess you could say we were pretty well off. My brother and I both had a chance to go to college and of course, you know about my stint at Princeton," Karl said. "I was lucky, I had a full scholarship."

Rose said, "You do you speak English well but you have a funny American accent."

"Yeah, I've been told that."

"What was your major in college," Rose asked.

"How's this for irony, history," he said with a laughing snort. "I guess we're making some of that now."

Rose said, "For better or worse."

"Yeah, you for better, me for worse."

"Yes, it appears you were fighting on the wrong side of history for a time but I believe it was very brave of you to come out of the darkness."

"My darling, that was the easy part, I just had to follow you."

Rose asked, "Do you have any hobbies, sports?"

"I play tennis pretty well and I like to ski."

"Well it appears we are perfect for each other. I love to ski and play tennis. Can't wait to do those things with you."

Karl said, "I'd love to. Maybe we'll get a chance to play before this God forsaken war is over. Okay, your turn, tell me about yourself."

"Well I guess I can start by telling you that I'm one quarter Jewish but you may have already known that."

"Yes, I've read that in your dossier."

"Okay, here's something I have not told you yet. My father was killed just three weeks ago as I was trying to lead him and others to safety over the mountains to Switzerland from Italy."

He asked, "How is that possible? You came to me in France just two weeks ago."

"You know, things happen fast in war. They didn't give me any time, just sent me to France to get you. They thought it was a milk run. Nobody knew I was going to run into that Gestapo butcher."

"Oh, my God, I am so sorry about your dad."

A single tear rolled down her face but she intercepted it and waved it off like it was no big deal. But of course, it was a very big deal. They took a moment in silence.

"Okay," she said, let me tell you the rest of the story."

She told him about her mother and twin sister living in the United States.

She told him about her father and his gangster prohibition business.

She told him about meeting her brother-in-law during Operation Torch.

"Did you know all that already. Been reading my dossier?" She asked.

No, I don't remember reading about any of that," he said.

Rose told him she was a wealthy young woman.

"So, I don't need this job working for British intelligence. They told me they needed me. But I've been doing this since before the war started and I need a break. Marry me and we can take a honeymoon in Scotland. You could wear a kilt for me."

"You know, if I stay here after the war is over, people are going to hate me. And if I go back to Germany, people are going to hate me. Can you live with that?"

"Yes, I can live with you on the moon. Because I'm in love with you but I'd really like to live in my home in Switzerland. Now no more excuses. Marry me."

"Yes, yes I will. I am the luckiest man in the world."

Karl disposed of his uniforms and with Rose, went shopping for a civilian wardrobe. There would be no going back for him.

Chapter 25

The Late July – August, 1944

The Allies on the Western Front broke out of the hedgerows of France, led by Patton's Third Army. A phalanx of Sherman tanks, backed by the allies' advantage of air cover, moved steadily across the country, freeing cities that had been under the gun of the Third Reich for years.

The Germans were finally in full retreat from Italy. The Soviets reached the border of East Prussia.

July 17, Rommel was badly injured when his driver lost control of their jeep, after being shot; attacked from above by two Canadian Spitfires.

On July 20, a little more than a month after D-Day, a bomb went off in Hitler's bunker in an attempt to kill the dictator. The attempt was unsuccessful.

Hitler ordered his generals to burn Paris to the ground. The order was ignored. On August 25, Paris was liberated by Free French troops backed by the American forces.

***

The newly engaged couple, Rose and Karl, traveled towards Len's airbase in southern England to meet with their closest family member and tell him their good news.

Len, knowing the area, picked the restaurant. Upon their arrival, Len gave Rose a hug and after introductions, shook hands with Karl. Len wore his uniform. Karl wore gray slacks and a light blue shirt. Rose matched him, with a light blue skirt, white shirt and gray scarf.

Len said, “I hope you like this place, it’s hard to find good food in England. These people seem to be allergic to spices. I figured a place with bangers and beans would be close enough to American hotdogs and Swiss sausage.” The three of them shared a laugh.

Rose said, “Close enough, the company’s more important than the food. How have you been?”

Len said, “I’ve been quite busy. My bomber squadron has attacked targets near and far in France and Germany.”

Karl said, “That sounds dangerous.”

“Yes, we’ve suffered some losses. Rose, I see you dyed your hair back to being blonde. Does that mean no more Clark Kent imitations on your travels behind enemy lines?”

Rose said, “You know that ‘loose lips sink ships’ saying, so I can’t tell you the details but on my last travels, as you call them, I watched my father get killed, was captured and escaped from a very bad man and brought Karl to England. So, I'm taking an extended leave and Karl and I are getting married."

Len said, "Wow, that's a lot to take in. Sorry to hear about your father. Does Iris know yet?"

"Well I wrote her, but you know how the mail works or doesn't work going across the Atlantic these days."

Len said, "Karl, you have a strange English accent, more American than English but what else, German?"

"He's from Berlin, but that's all we are allowed to tell you."

Len said, "Oh hush hush spy stuff, so intriguing. Let me guess, you were spying on Hitler. Right?"

Karl said, "Sorry mate, I'm not allowed to talk about it. You'll have to wait till the war is over to find out all the details."

Len said, “Rose, with your hair blonde, you look so much like my wife. I don’t suppose you’d lend her to me for a night would you Karl? Please don’t get upset, just kidding.”

Rose laughed, “Sounds like some dates Iris and I had when we were in high school. Don’t get upset Len, just kidding.”

“When’s the big date?” Len asked.

“Tomorrow, London City Hall, can you come?”

“I’m truly sorry, I can’t. You know, duty calls. But congratulations, all my best.”

After scarfing down bangers and beans, they hugged their goodbyes.

Chapter 26

August – September, 1944

General Rommel was implicated in the attack on Hitler's bunker, while he remained hospitalized from his injuries.

German V-1 and V-2 rockets hit London.

The Allies executed Operation Market Garden, as thousands of airborne troops jumped into the Netherlands and liberated the country.

***

Rose and Karl were wed on August 25, the day Paris was liberated.

They had just finished their vows when without warning the building across the street from them exploded. Both bride and groom were knocked to the ground. Rose's simple white wedding dress was covered with black coal dust and gray dirt, her face covered with soot, but luckily both of them were unhurt.

She yelled, "What the bloody hell was that!"

Karl's ears rang and he couldn't hear her but he grabbed her hand and ushered her away from the street which was becoming chaotic. People hurt, on the ground, in the street screaming for help. One lady ran by, her clothing on fire. Body parts littered the rubble.

It was the first explosion of Hitler's miracle weapon that he hoped to win the war with, the V-2 Rocket. Unlike the primitive V-1 which was fired from an aircraft, this newer, more sophisticated weapon was launched behind German lines and traveled faster than the speed of sound, the only warning being the sonic boom in the air.

Karl and Rose spent the rest of their wedding day bandaging wounds and attending to life threatening injuries; doing triage as ambulances came and went.

In the early evening too exhausted and weary to change their clothes, they caught a sleeper car to begin their honeymoon in Scotland.

No sooner had they checked into their hotel when a telegram arrived for Rose. She opened it expecting congratulations. Instead her mother said,

"I FORBID YOU FROM MARRYING THAT NAZI!"

Rose was livid. She thought, the nerve of that woman.

She sent the reply:

My husband Karl is not a Nazi. Stop

That is all I can tell you. Stop

Thank you for your wedding wishes. Stop

Rose had been ambushed twice on her wedding day; yet she was determined to make her honeymoon special for herself and her new husband.

He proudly wore a kilt on their first wedded night and she was excited with the thought of him not wearing underwear. But try as she might she couldn't get her mother's telegram off her mind. In the middle of dinner, she broke down and cried.

Karl put his arms around her. He thought she was reacting to the explosion. He said, "It'll be alright darling. The Allies will soon win this war."

With that, she showed him the telegram.

He expected to get ostracized for being in the German army but he had not expected it from her family.

"I'm sorry," he said.

"Dammit! Karl, it's not you who should be saying you're sorry. My mother has always thought she was so noble. She treated my father with the same kind of disrespect, ruining her marriage. Now she's trying to ruin mine, but we won't let her will we Karl? If she can't treat you with respect, I won't have anything to do with her."

The next day she called Professor Sutterhand and read her mother's telegram to him.

Rose said, "It would appear that we have some sort of a breach in our secret proceedings."

"Rose, do you know what Karl's in country status is?"

"What do you mean?"

"Well, you are in this country on a student visa."

"That makes sense."

"Karl's status is a POW and his status is not classified. Anyone can check someone's status."

"But why a POW?"

"Well of course, we could not list him as a spy."

Rose fumed, “But a POW…?”

“I’m sorry Rose, but we are at war. There is no other way to explain his presence here,” the Professor said. “If it weren’t for you marrying him, nobody would be interested in his status at all.”

“Is there any way you can talk to my mother and help rectify the situation?”

He said, “I’ll see what I can do.”

Two days later the Professor contacted Rose. “Can you be here at headquarters by 1600?”

“Professor, you know I’m in Scotland on my honeymoon.”

The professor said, “That’s why I got you a ride. There’s transport waiting for you to bring you back to London. I want you to know I did this for you,” he told her.

“Great, thank you.”

Back at headquarters the radioman said, "This radio is really powerful. It will work for you just like a telephone. I've got your mom on the phone, go ahead."

The radioman pulled the telephone style receiver out of the radio box and handed it to her.

"Hello Rose. Are you there?" Katherine asked.

"Hello Mother."

"Rose it is unconscionable that you would marry a Nazi. I won't stand for it," her mother said indignantly.

Rose said, "Karl is not a Nazi. I am not at liberty to tell you the whole story but I've been fighting Nazi's this whole war. I know Nazis."

Katherine said, "Well don't marry him until we can get him all checked out."

"Mother, you have no right to tell me who I can marry," Rose said her temper starting to boil. "While you were safe in America, thanks to my father and me, if you remember, I've been here doing my part in the war effort."

Her mother said, "We've been doing our part too. I'm a volunteer at the Red Cross."

Rose laughed at her. "You think raising money for the Red Cross is comparable to those fighting the war?"

"No, of course not. You were busy getting your father killed. Iris' husband is in the Army Air Corps."

"I know, he is here in England and we talked two days ago. Len is wonderful. You know nothing about what happened with my dad and unfortunately I can't talk about it, it's still classified."

"So, the great Nazi fighter is not allowed to talk about anything. How convenient. I am warning you Rose, don't marry the Nazi," Katherine told her.

Rose said, "You are so infuriating and so wrong. I'm already married to Karl. His status has been changed from POW to British Military. He is a complex person, you don't have to concern yourself about, because I refuse to have any more dealings with you. Is Iris there? I'd like to talk to her"

"Iris, unlike you, will do what I tell her. She has always been a good daughter. You can write her a letter. Goodbye Rose."

The line went dead.

Chapter 27

October – December, 1944

The V-2 rockets continued to fall on Britain at a rate of eight a day. It was a case of too little, too late, to make a significant difference in the war.

Rommel was implicated in the attack on Hitler's bunker. Although Rommel opposed assassinating Hitler, he agreed to demand that Hitler step down.

When the plot came to light, Hitler knew it would be a major scandal to have the popular 'folk hero' Rommel publicly branded as a traitor.

He gave Rommel the option of suicide by cyanide or a public trial, tantamount to a death sentence.

General Erwin Rommel took the poison after learning that his death would be listed as having occurred from "natural causes" and that his family would be provided for.

He was given a state funeral.

***

Franklin Roosevelt was elected to a fourth term as President of the United States.

General George Patton's tank division crossed into Germany.

Hitler played a last gamble and launched the Battle of the Bulge in Belgium which met with early success. The Americans refused to surrender the surrounded city of Bastogne. When the German general asked the U.S. Commander, General McAuliffe to give up; his reply was, "Nuts."

As a heavy fog cleared, Allied aircraft unleashed an attack on the German tanks and turned the American predicament into a victory.

***

Karl awoke on the morning of December 10th after a bad dream. He turned to Rose and said, "I need to see the Professor, I know what he is going to do."

Rose said, "You know what who is going to do?"

"Hitler."

"How in the world do you know what that madman is going to do?"

"He talked about it in a meeting with Rommel last year before D-day. It's his last-ditch plan to turn defeat into victory, and it came back to me in a dream. I've got to tell the Professor before it's too late."

"Okay," she said, "I'll get you a meeting."

Karl described to Sutterhand and MI6, Hitler's plan to drive a wedge of new Tiger tanks between the

English and American forces, cutting them off from each other, in a last chance attack toward the Belgian Port of Antwerp to keep the allies from using the harbor to supply the troops.

The Professor relayed Karl's concerns to Eisenhower.

Sutterhand said, "Ike replied, said he's been hearing rumors of a German offensive but thinks it is a ruse to move Patton's Third Army back from the German Border, to keep Patton's tanks from making a New Year's break out into the heart of Germany."

"But he will heed your warning and keep the veteran 101st Airborne on the front lines, instead of relieving them before Christmas."

The Battle of the Bulge played out just as Karl predicted. Only the presence of the 101st Airborne kept Bastogne from being overrun and Patton's Tanks were sent to relieve the squeeze on McAuliffe's men.

Eisenhower awarded Ramstein another medal.

Of course it was all kept secret until after the war.

***

Rose tried to turn Karl's rejection by her mother into a victory. She started by sending a long letter to her sister. She asked Iris to reserve judgment about Karl until the war was over. She could present all the facts about the situation when it was declassified and she could talk openly.

The newlyweds made a date with Len for lunch. Rose and Karl drove through the foggy English countryside back to the rustic restaurant where they ate with him the last time.

They were a bit early so they got a table and waited, and waited. After two hours Len still did not show up. They went to his base and asked for him. An army captain wearing a frown greeted them.

A moment of dread attacked Rose. No please, no!

"I'm Len's CO, Captain Rogers, who are you?" he asked.

"I'm Rose, Len's sister in law." She showed him her identification.

"I guess, you being family, I can tell you…Len's plane was shot down over Germany yesterday. He is MIA. I'm so sorry."

"MIA," Rose said. "So, he might be alive?"

"Yes, he might," the Captain said, "but there were no parachutes seen by the squadron before the plane fell. Sorry."

Dizziness tore at Rose and she leaned against Karl for support. "Have you sent a telegram to my sister yet?"

"Yes ma'am, I took care of that personally. Again, I'm so sorry."

Karl led her away. As they marched back to the car, Rose's head felt shrouded in a thick fog.

She said, "Somehow, my mother will probably blame this on me."

Chapter 28

1939 – 1946

St. Louis, Missouri

A strange thing happened to Katherine Wineheim after she moved to the United States. She fell in love with her absentee husband. Surrounded by the Cohen family and their heritage, Katherine slowly adapted their traditions. To her adopted family's surprise she and her daughter, Iris, converted to Judaism and even learned some Yiddish.

Katherine gave her maiden name of Wineheim to her soon to be quite successful beer, making sure the American public knew it was from an old Austrian recipe, not German. Each can or bottle of Wineheim beer had a picture of Iris dressed like a

Disney Princess complete with crown, on one side, and stately Katherine looking like an elder Queen Victoria on the other.

In the days before television advertisements, this label became very important to the Wineheim brand. It showed beauty and class. The product blew off the shelves becoming second only to that other St. Louis brewery.

When Marc was killed in Italy, Katherine took it hard. She somehow hoped after the war she and Marc might get back together. She put on her best black dress, ripped the garment and sat Shiva.

Iris had always been close to her mother and she underwent a very different metamorphosis, marrying the Jewish boy, Len, from New York. After his plane went down, she lit a yahrzeit candle for him before the war ended.

She learned after Len left for war that she carried his child.

Iris met Len's older brother Jake, after he was discharged from the Navy. Circumstance threw them together and after Iris gave birth to Len Junior, Jake fell in love with his brother's widow.

Rose and Karl were not invited to the wedding.

Chapter 29

January - May 1945

The German Army now desperately fighting for their own land used desperate tactics. Teenagers and old men joined what was left of Third Reich's defenses to face the brunt of the Allied invasion.

Patton's forces punched deep into Hitler's Fatherland. Despite efforts of the SS and Gestapo to cover up evidence of the Holocaust, their attempts were unsuccessful.

Concentration camps were uncovered one by one by the invading armies of Soviets, British and Americans. As the details of the death camps were revealed, even the war veterans who believed they had seen the worst evils of man could not believe what they discovered.

Eight million Jews, Gypsies, homosexuals, Seventh Day Adventists, Mormons, intellectuals, and others who spoke out against Hitler's regime were put to death. Many young women were forced into prostitution or slavery. Children too young to work, and feble elderly, were sent directly into gas chambers. The evil of the Nazis came into the light of day and humanity found the cruelty inconceivable.

How could it have happened? There is a famous quote that begins to explain how a society could let it take place:

"When they came for the Jews, I did nothing because I wasn't Jewish. When they came for the Gypsies I did nothing because I wasn't a Gypsy.

When they came for the homosexuals, I did nothing because I wasn't a homosexual. When they came for the intellectuals, I did nothing because I wasn't an intellectual. When they came for me no one was left to object." ~ anonymous

***

Back at Oxford, Rose ran into Lily Atwood.

"Wow Rose I haven't seen you in a couple of years"

"Well I've been quite busy, you know there's a war on," Rose replied.

Lily said, "Yes, me too. Do you have time to get some lunch?"

"Yes I do, just give me a minute I need to go to the bathroom."

Despite Lily's attempts to hide it, Rose saw her tattoo again as the girl pulled up her bloomers.

Rose said, "I'll take you to an Indian restaurant, my treat, let's splurge and take a taxi."

The food smelled delicious as they entered the restaurant. Scents of curry, coriander and turmeric punctuated the air. Deep rich purple walls and authentic Indian décor made Rose feel like she had been transported to a foreign world. Thoughts of a visit to see this British Colony crossed her mind.

Lily said, "I can't believe it, I have to go to the bathroom again, too much tea I guess. I'll be right back."

While Lily was gone Rose thought about that tattoo on Lily's upper thigh and a revelation slapped her in the face.

The young lady she helped to freedom sat again at the table. Rose said, "Lily, you seem to have a weird tattoo on your leg, did it say Frank and Lily forever with two lightning bolts? Isn't that the sign of the SS?"

Lily reached into her purse, pulled out a gun and pointed it at Rose under the table. “You weren’t supposed to see that,” she said. “Don’t move a muscle I’ve got a gun on you.”

Rose said, “Have you been a double agent all along?”

“Bingo! You’re such a smart cookie. We’re going to walk out of here slowly,” Lily said.

Rose said, “You were probably the one who had us chased by those Nazis that I wiped out in the avalanche. It was you who told Sargent Schmidt where to find me.”

“Right again, Frank Schmidt was my step-brother and my lover.” Lily said, “Now move.”

Rose said, “I don’t think so.”

Lily said, “What are you going to do? Stop me with your Swiss army knife?”

"No actually while you were in the bathroom, I traded guns with you, the one you have has no bullets."

Lily pulled the trigger, nothing happened.

Rose said, "Now our roles are reversed and I will be happy to kill you if I have to. We're going to go see the Professor and you're going to confess."

Lily said, "Over my dead body."

"Okay have it your way." Rose pulled the trigger.

Blood bloomed across Lily's shoulder, and stained Lily's dress. The gun blast drew everyone's attention.

Rose yelled to the waiter, "Call the police immediately!" She turned to Lily, "Don't you move, we'll stay and wait for the police, I will shoot you again if I have to."

Lily, showing her true colors, said, "You Jew bitch! I should have killed you as soon as I saw you."

When the police arrived, Rose showed them her ID and said, “Please call MI6 for me, ask for Professor Sutterhand.” She handed the police officer her gun.

An ambulance arrived and the medic attended to Lily’s wound.

Maybe I should have killed her. Some people are plain evil, Rose thought. Lily can’t be saved. I guess I’ll let a jury decide.

Chapter 30

April – May 1945

Hitler hid deep in his Berlin bunker. But after hearing news of Mussolini in Italy captured by partisans, strung up and mutilated with his mistress; the Fuhrer chose to take poison with Eva Braun, who he married hours earlier.

***

The Professor called Rose and Karl back to intelligence headquarters at Oxford.

"I have one last important job for you Karl. I would like you to join in with the German high command as part of the peace conference. The Soviets in taking Berlin, have an advantage over the British and the Americans. Karl, you could be very helpful to the negotiation process."

Karl said, "Sorry Professor, I'm never wearing that uniform again and I wish I never had."

Rose said, "It appears the British, Americans and the Soviet Union are trying to figure out how to fight the next war. I want no part of it."

"My war is over. It's time for me to take my husband to Switzerland and neutrality," Rose declared.

***

Rose and Karl took the ferry across the Channel to Antwerp where they caught the train. Flags of the

United States, Belgium, France and Switzerland flew above the locomotive's engine, but the swastika of Nazi Germany had been torn down. The train chugged on its last leg of the trip from Belgium through bombed out Germany. Rose studied the mess that had once been Munich from her window.

When shots rang out the train screeched to a halt. Armed American soldiers assigned to ride the rails grabbed guns and went to defend the transportation line.

Karl said, "We need to curtail this before it gets out of control, I'll take the German home guard group. You take the Allied's side."

"Yes, I think that's best," Rose said.

The two followed Allied soldiers off the train and put themselves between the rivals.

Karl yelled "HALT! Stop! What are you doing? Hitler is dead. Lay your guns down. No more Killing.

Rose put herself in front of the Allies. "Don't Shoot. They are just a ragtag group of old men and young boys. Enough Killing."

The leader of the home guard asked Karl, "Who the hell are you?" He answered, "I am Major Ramstein staff advisor to General Rommel. Now put your hands up and throw down your weapons. Damn it! Do it NOW!

The home guard leader of the Germans looked at the line of Allied men and said, "Do it."

His followers laid down their guns, many of which looked like they had last seen action in World War I. The group of Germans dispersed.

The Captain, leader of the Allied troops came over to Rose and Karl and said, "I've never seen anything like that. What bravery. You two deserve a medal."

Rose said, "We are just tired of all the killing."

After everyone re-boarded the train, the conductor sounded the horn, engaged the engine and moved towards the mountains ahead.

Rose said to Karl, “You were very brave there.”

Karl said, “Very brave or stupid?’

Rose laughed, “Maybe brave and stupid.”

Chapter 31

May 7, 1945

V-E Day

Victory in Europe arrived as Germany unconditionally surrendered. Certain countries of Europe staged a great celebration muted somewhat with their armies still fighting in the Pacific. Even neutral Switerland joined in the contented mood of cease fire on their home continent.

***

Rose and Karl retreated to her childhood home in Zurich. The house Rose and her Dad mostly lived in during her teen years.

The spacious house could be called elegant, but it's lack of pretension gave it an air of comfort.

Photographs of Switzerland's gorgeous mountains and countryside adorned the walls. May flowers grew in the garden, bathing the house in color. The surrounding mountains created a spectacular view from the home's many windows.

Three Swiss employees had keep up the family home for Rose and her father throughout the war, the female cook, the man Friday and the gardener.

They had been informed by letter about Marc Cohen's death. Having been employed by the business for years, they felt like they were part of the family and took the news hard.

But Rose was unhappy with the way they treated her husband, making fun of his Berlin accent. She called them into a meeting with Karl.

Rose told them, "You have been faithful employees for years for my father and me. That is the only reason I have not fired you. Karl is my husband, and your new boss. Take the next two weeks off with pay, you deserve it. But when you come back, I expect you to show him your total respect and loyalty. Otherwise you are free to find other employment. So, how many of you want to keep your jobs?"

All three agreed to her conditions.

"Good," Rose said, "we will see you in two weeks. Enjoy yourselves."

Rose turned to Karl, "Finally we are alone at home. We have much to celebrate. The good guys won and we helped. What a relief. I feel like I can finally breathe."

"Come over here Karl. I've taken this seven-year-old bottle of Champagne from the wine cellar and chilled it. I've been saving it for this special day of celebration. This bubbly's from before this whole mess started."

Rose popped the cork and they drank right out of the bottle. The bubbles made them burp and they got the giggles.

“Come on Foxy, let's celebrate,” he laughed. “How did that kid’s American expression go? “Whistle while you work. Hitler is a jerk. Mussolini bit his weenie, now it doesn't squirt.”

Rose laughed ‘till tears ran down her face. “That's the best laugh I’ve had in a long time.”

Some of the sparkling wine spilled and washed over them. It felt good.

Rose said, “My darling we have all the time in the world. We’re finally home.”

She stepped back and unbuttoned her shirt revealing a lacy black bra underneath. She tantalizingly undressed, outer garments falling to the floor.

Karl paused for a moment to admire his goddess.

Only the all powerful God of the Hebrews could make something this gorgeous. He drew a deep breath taking in the scent of her and sighed. She stood, a lovely contradiction of contrasts. The black frilly panties highlighting porcelain white skin. Her sunshine golden hair above twin Lake Lucerne eyes, so deep blue he wanted to dive into them and become part of Rose forever.

She had hard abdominal muscles below soft breasts that stood high like peaks of Swiss mountains, and hard nipples, ready for his love.

Even the slight imperfection, the little crook to her otherwise button-nose, she wore well; as a badge to her bravery.

This woman, with a face so beautiful it could launch a thousand battleships. Her face had come to him in dreams on cold nights in the North African Desert. Only this goddess could give him the courage to do the right thing–come out of the cold and follow her to the Allied side.

Karl said, “You look incredible. You have been my fantasy woman since the first time I saw you in that French Cafe in Nancy. I love you so much.”

The White Fox smiled her sexy smile and said, “Shut up and kiss me.”

He kissed that spot behind her neck tenderly as he had that first time together. He kissed his way down her body stopping and lingering at her breasts. She shivered in his arms.

They made love slowly, tenderly, exploring each other, discovering what gave their partner pleasure. After reaching orgasm together, they lay back in passionate bliss.

From the bedroom window they watched fireworks explode high above the city. They drank more champagne and started all over again.

Chapter 32

May 1945

Rose and Karl awoke the next morning hungover and sexually satisfied.

Rose made a breakfast of sausage and eggs that smelled and tasted like heaven, compared to the awful powdered eggs they ate during the war.

She said between mouthfuls, "It feels strange being in this big house all alone with you. I'm a little lonely. No offense my love. I desperately miss my father, my sister, and I even miss the evil witch of the Midwest—my mother."

"I have an idea, tell me what you think. There are many Jewish orphans at the Swiss Camps. How would you feel about adopting, a girl for me and a boy for you?"

Karl said, "I think it's a great idea."

They drove to an orphanage and were introduced to many children. A brother and sister caught their eye and shyly smiled back at them. It was love at first sight. They sat down and played with the youngsters for a while and Rose asked, "How would you two like to come home with us?"

"That would be all right," Deborah said, bright brown eyes shining.

Karl said, "That would make us very happy."

Two days later, five-year-old Deborah and four-year-old David were riding back to Zurich with their adoptive parents.

Karl said to Rose, "They are Jewish and we should respect that and raise them that way. Let's join the local synagogue."

Karl and Rose converted and raised the children in the Jewish faith.

Chapter 33

May 1946

Nuremberg, Germany

Certain notorious Nazi's were put on trial for crimes against humanity.

***

Karl's father, Arthur Ramstein, was indicted and tried on multiple counts of murder and kidnapping. He had been in charge of slave laborers working on the V2 rocket. After a guilty verdict, he killed himself by taking an overdose of sleeping pills.

Karl quietly changed his name from Ramstein to Cohen.

Chapter 34

Switzerland 1965

As adults David and Deborah married outside their religion and their families left Judaism behind. Karl shaken by this rejection asked them why?

Their answer surprised him. "Dad," Debbie said, "I believe you raised us Jewish to satisfy some guilt you felt about World War II, but we didn't need your guilt, just your love. And we got that."

David said, "I don't want to be Jewish. Don't get me wrong, I know it was the religion of my ancestors but if a religion believes theirs is right, all the others must be wrong. There have been too many religious wars in history. I like being Swiss and our heritage of neutrality."

Karl and Rose were disappointed but accepted their children's choices.

Chapter 35

July 2018

Roger, Sara and Rose were served what had become the college kids favorite meal over the summer. The cook, Sandra, filled their plates with her special family recipe of goulash. As usual it smelled delicious and tasted even better.. They ate outside, on the patio of Rose's garden at her home in Zurich. The Alps provided the backdrop.

Roger Raintree asked Rose, "Did you think Karl knew about the Holocaust during the war?"

Rose answered, "He had suspicions, he knew the SS and the Gestapo were rounding up Jews. His father had slave laborers working for him and was involved with developing the V2 Rocket. But Karl never knew about that, it was top secret.

"Ironically, Karl's mother was killed in Berlin when Len, my brother-in-law was shot down. The Professor told me that little tidbit."

"Karl died in 2001. He was the love of my life and I miss him every day."

"Unlike my mother, I never blamed him for the Holocaust. He and I talked about it. He realized that I took him to England and probably saved his life. I couldn't save him from my mother's wrath. To her he was evil incarnate.

I can tell you that he felt tremendous guilt about fighting on the wrong side. But he didn't think that evil was only a German thing. Karl knew his history too well. Throughout history evil often prevailed, like slavery in the United States and the British during the Boer Wars in South Africa.

He believed that we all have good and bad residing in us, like *Dr. Jekyll and Mr. Hyde* and it was up to all of us to choose the good over the evil."

Sara, Rose's great niece asked, "Did you ever see my great-grandmother, Iris again?"

"Yes, actually I did. I went to our mother Katherine's funeral in St.Louis. We met privately and buried the hatchet and kissed each other goodbye. But she never lost her animosity towards Karl, so, I stayed away."

"When Karl died, Iris came to Switzerland for a couple of weeks and we had some fun together. That was the last time I saw her."

Roger changing the subject. "Hey Rose, how can you tell the Swiss haven't fought in a war for a long time."

Rose said, "I don't know, tell me."

"Their most important weapon is the Swiss Army knife."

They all laughed.

Rose said, “I like that one even though I heard it before.”

Sara remarked, “We need to get the two Cohen families together. My side would love to meet you and your family.”

Rose said, “I would love to host all of you here in Switzerland. We should do it soon while the weather is still nice. You are all invited.”

Chapter 36

August 2018

The Cohen family get together occurred on a bright and sunny summer's day. Puffy cumulus clouds dotted the mountain sky.

Although not directly related, Roger's family was included as honorary Cohen//s and they were all invited to the party at Rose's home in Zurich.

Including Rose, there were five generations of the combined Cohen clan at the outdoor barbecue.

Champagne and beer flowed like spring creeks in the surrounding mountains. The Kosher food was plentiful and delicious. There were bagels, with cream cheese, smoked salmon and red onions and assorted knishes Barbecued brisket and hot pastrami ladled into fresh baked rolls. Fresh vegetable and fruit salads were set on each table with floral centerpieces.

The weather cooperated; brilliant sunshine beamed down on the combined Cohen family, amid stunning views of the mountains.

Rose pulled Roger and Sara aside. "Come sit by me," she said. "I hear your book about me has found an agent, congratulations."

"I want to ask you something. Did you two ever think of dating? You're such a cute couple," Rose told them.

Roger groaned, turning scarlet, "But we're best friends. We've been best friends forever."

Rose said, "Don't you know, best friends make the best couples? Love comes and goes, but best friends are forever."

Sara, also a bright shade of red said, “Do you know Rose, when I came to see you, I had no idea that we would become friends. I’m so proud to have such a ‘badass’ war hero in my family. I have honestly fallen in love with you.”

Roger said, “That’s one thing we can agree on right now. I’ve fallen in love with you too. How much older are you than me?”

The White Fox giggled.

Roger and Sara laughed together.

Rose confessed, “One of the problems of outliving all my friends is I’ve been lonely. My children and grandchildren are off living their lives and I’m happy for them. But you two have kept me company and busy this summer. So, I want to invite you to come here and ski on your Christmas Vacation.”

Sara looked at Roger and shrugged her shoulders. “Go ahead and tell her.”

Roger said, “We have a special surprise for you. The chairman of the History Department at Oxford realized your Professor made a promise to you that you would get college credit while working for MI6. I have your diploma. Also, they have awarded two scholarships in your name. So, Sara and I will be attending college in England this Fall and we can come visit often. What do you think of that?”

Rose said, “I’m so happy.” Tears ran down her face.”

Sara said, “Roger it appears my *badass* Aunt Rose has a soft side.”

End

Acknowledgements for **White Fox Blues:**

A World War II Woman's Spy Story

I would like to thank Ana Manwaring and her writing class for their input on my drafts for this book.

Thanks to Cathy Carsel my main editor and proof reader.

A thank you goes to Juliet Vonturi for her help.

They all had big parts in bringing this exciting novel of historic fiction to life.

As a high school history teacher for over thirty years, I feel it is important to share knowledge with others about the history of the World.

In my own way I have attempted to carry out this important tradition.

My first attempt at this endeavor took place in Tony White's Writing Historical Fiction class at Sonoma State University n the early 1970's. It was Tony who led me to believe I had something to share and had the ability to do it. Yet I would take thirty years to produce my first book:

Rumors About my Father, about. Leo Winters, U.S. Navy, fought in WWII and drove a landing craft at Omaha Beach on D-Day.

Soon after, in Saint Helena I met 92-year-old Iola Hitt in a writing class and she needed me to write her World War II story:

No Place for a Wallflower was the product of that work we did together. She was so proud of that book that she carried it everywhere until she passed away four years later.

I have written and published 15 books of prose and poetry in the last 12 years.

I hope you enjoy the thrilling spy story:

White Fox Blues

A World War Woman's II Spy Story

About the Author

Nathaniel Robert (Bob) Winters was born in Brooklyn, grew up on Long Island, New York, and is a U.S. Navy Vietnam Veteran.

Nathaniel earned a BA in history, with honors, from Sonoma State University, in California.

He achieved a Masters in education from California State University, Stanislaus.

Mr. Winters has written and published fifteen books of different genres including historical fiction, biography, science fiction, mystery, young adult and poetry.

He lives in the Napa Valley, California.

His previous World War II history books include two biographies:

Rumors About my Father and No Place for a Wallflower

Other books by Nathaniel Robert Winters:

The Legend of Heath Angelo: about the man who founded the first Nature Preserve in CA.

Penngrove Ponderosa: fiction about coming home from Vietnam and college years

Seventh Grade Blues: a Young Adult mystery and prequel to *White Fox WWII Blues*

Finding Shelter from the Cold: How wolves became dogs in the ice age

The Poet I did not Know: Poetry

Another Revolution: Poetry

Not Quite Kosher: a memoir

The Adventures of the Omaha Kid: Baseball, tennis and lots of romance

Heavenly Bodies and Other Diversions: Short Stories Poems and more.

Made in the USA
Middletown, DE
27 September 2022

11193382R00111